Ménage à Noir

Other Works by Steven Hartov

The Last of the Seven
The Soul of a Thief
Afghanistan on the Bounce
The Night Stalkers
In the Company of Heroes
The Devil's Shepherd
The Nylon Hand of God
The Heat of Ramadan

Visit www.stevenhartov.com
for more on the author and his work.

Ménage à Noir

3 Short Stories
by
STEVEN HARTOV

ISBN-13 (Paperback): 978-1-965364-00-0

ISBN-13 (E-Book): 978-1-965364-01-7

Ménage à Noir

Copyright © 2024 by Steven Hartov

All rights reserved. This book or any portion thereof may not be reproduced or used in any manner whatsoever without written permission of the publisher, except for the use of brief quotations embedded in critical articles or reviews.

This is a work of fiction. Names, characters, places, or incidents are either the product of the author's imagination or are used in a fictitious manner. Any resemblance to actual persons, living or dead, businesses, companies, events, or locals is purely coincidental.

4pm Press
www.4pm.press

Printed in USA

Media inquiries or copy usage should be directed to the media representative:

Lis Malone Media

lis@lismalone.com / vwww.lismalone.com

For all the scribblers, keyboard bandits, midnight hair pullers, hard drinkers, tale weavers and dreamers who never gave up.

Author Note

Writers are made, not born.

Some are natural storytellers, those kids who could weave a tale of imagination and enthrall their friends in the shadows and sparks of a summer campfire. Some are voracious readers, the ones who buried themselves under a blanket and used a flashlight to summon pages upon pages of literary adventures. Yet no writer arrives in this world with the magical skills required to devise compelling plots, dramatic structure, and memorable characters. Much like the journeys of sculptors, those things come only with years of practice, sweat, stubborn determination, and broken stone.

My writer's journey began as a boy in New England, parented by a mother and father who imparted the gifts of history, music, and literature. Like most of my peers I burned through comic books and all of The Hardy Boys mysteries, then begged my encouraging mother for more mature fiction. Soon I was reading Alistair MacLean,

James A. Michener, F. Scott Fitzgerald, Leon Uris, and a writer I came to idolize, Ernest Hemingway.

I suppose I knew, early on, that I was going to become a writer. Yet I also understood from those marvelous tracts of adventure literature, that in order for a writer to make his work seem real, he had to know something about the real world, firsthand. And so began my personal adventures, from which I knew – if indeed I survived – that my writer's well would then be brimming with the sights, sounds, smells, and colors that an author needs in order for his work to jump off the page.

Halfway through my college education, I dropped out, joined the US Merchant Marine and sailed the seven seas, winding up in the Middle East in the midst of a war. I returned to finish up my degree yet knew that my appetite for adventure had only been whetted for more. Hailing from a family of Holocaust survivors, I joined the IDF as a paratrooper, then moved on to intelligence and special operations, filling my writer's well with a generous cast of characters, exotic locales, and near fatal forays. Finally, back in the United States, I was nearly thirty-years-old before I felt my pencil had been sharpened enough by fire that I might have something to say.

These three stories in Ménage à Noir are of a certain style, a bit on the dark side, hence the moniker "noir." Dead Drop evolved from another of my youthful pursuits, SCUBA diving, as well as my experiences in the Caribbean islands and some rough men and women I've known. The Other End of Newbury Street, an early story I penned while residing in Boston, is a character sketch with a twist, which I honed further much later on. Pocket Litter developed from my brief but memorable service as an Army Intelligence Operator and explores the dangerous deeds engaged in by my popular protagonists, Eytan Eckstein and Benjamin Baum, from my espionage trilogy that began with The Heat of Ramadan.

All of the characters in this collection are based on people I know or have known, with respectable alterations in their names and descriptions. When capturing foreign accents or features, I write what I hear and see, without intent to offend, but also without self-censorship. Political correctness may be the new norm, but it is the slaughter of truth, and I am past the age of participation.

I hope that you, my readers, will enjoy these places and people. Much as I did myself, when I saw them, met them, and captured them all.

—Steven Hartov

1. DEAD DROP

JEAN RENÉ DUBOIS drove down Front Street in a fairly new Renault touring van, the kind that has big windows all around and seats twelve with the extra fold-down buckets. The main thoroughfare of Philipsburg, capital of the Dutch side of the island of St. Maarten, glistened with a light wash of morning rain. The tall palms that shaded the small hotels and cafés on the beach side leaned in over the narrow street, vaguely resisting a stiff breeze blowing in from Great Bay.

It had been blowing like that for three straight days. The big catamarans that usually ran tourists to St. Barts, Anguilla, and Saba lay sail-less in their moorings, their small crews kicking aimlessly at the idle lines and stays.

It was too early for the tourist shops to open and there were only a few black Antilleans in the street. Two of them were fishermen and one was a heavy woman pushing a shopping cart full of green bananas. Three small children in tan uniforms ran down Front Street, late for school at the big white church in the center of town.

Dubois parked the van in front of a small building on the north side of the street away from the beach front. There was a blue and white plastic sign that said *Epstein's Guest House* rocking back and forth over the street. With all the beautiful beach resorts scattered around the island, Epstein's was clearly not for the well-heeled tourist.

Dubois got out and pushed his straw fedora back on his head. He walked around to the front of the Renault and frowned at the mud-spattered license plate. Then he spit on his brown fingers, bent over and carefully cleaned the orange-yellow plate so the words could be clearly seen. ST. MAARTEN — THE FRIENDLY ISLAND.

A bell tinkled and the door to Epstein's opened, and Dubois stood up and smiled. He had an endearing grin, made more so by the fact that the soft flesh of the inside of his thick upper lip always stuck to his big white teeth.

"Good mornin' Meester Harris," Dubois sang in the deep French accent of his native Martinique.

"Morning, Jean."

J.D. Harris stood in the open doorway. He was a big man, pushing forty, with a full head of coarse brown hair and a lot of muscle left on his college ballplayer's body. His upper lip was mottled red where he'd just shaved away a full moustache.

"Give me a hand, will ya?"

They slid back the side door of the Renault and carefully deposited Harris' diving gear – a 72 cubic foot tank with the old-style rubber backpack, a buoyancy compensator vest with CO_2 inflator, and his regulator, fins, mask, and snorkel. Harris made sure that his tank wouldn't roll around and he and Dubois slid into the front.

They drove down Front Street until they got to the Little Pier and took a left down Wilhelmina Hendrik, a narrow lane next to the post office where all the brass mailboxes for the whole town were outside along one wall. They took another left past the police station and headed west on Back Street and out of town.

They skirted the big inland Salt Pond, as large as a New England lake, and Harris stared at the spindly white cranes picking at the bugs in the shallow marshes. It didn't take much brains to figure he was not in a talky mood, but Dubois wasn't going to let that stop him from trying to cheer up his "boss".

"Hope you had a goood breakfast today, Meester Harris." Dubois grinned at the American.

"It's J.D.," Harris corrected.

"Oh no, sir. Nooo. I work for you now, so I am Jean, and you are Meester Harris. When you work for me then you will be J.D. and I will be Meester Dubois."

Harris smiled despite his mood. He still couldn't get used to the friendly and sometimes servile nature of St. Maartens' black natives. He liked Jean, but he was vaguely uncomfortable around him. He wondered if there might be a volcano beneath that surface of ebony calm.

"Well," said Harris, "I didn't overdo it this morning. Just a couple eggs and coffee. I'm not too good out at sea. At least not on the surface."

Dubois frowned. "But I think you were once in Navy, n'est ce pas?"

"Yeah. That's where I learned to puke. That's also why I got into the diving, real fast. Nice and calm down below, no matter what hell's blowing up top."

Dubois didn't quite understand all the fast English, but he kept up the chatter.

"So now, weather has been real too bad these few days. Make the tourists very sad. Tourists sad, we sad too."

They made a left after the Salt Pond and headed over the mountains toward the western side of the island and Mullet Bay. Harris was still too quiet for Dubois, who only enjoyed his work for the contact with people.

"I know it real hard on you, Meester Harris, you losing your partner and all. But maybe we find him today yet. Maybe he just went someplace nobody knows."

Harris pulled a pack of Camels from his shirt pocket and lit up with a match. He rolled down his window, leaned his thick elbow on it and looked down at the sea and some distant white caps. "Yeah, Jean. That's what I'm afraid of. He went someplace nobody knows."

J.D. Harris and Arthur Chester went way back, as far back as the U.S. Navy in the early seventies. They had started out in the service together, but neither of them much liked straight sea duty, so they got themselves transferred to diving school and hull maintenance. That was interesting enough for Harris, but Chester wanted more action. He got it with an Underwater Demolition Team and one last tour in Vietnam before they shut down the war.

After Nam, the two New Yorkers hooked back up again and opened a private investigations business in the city, putting their diving expertise to use on cases involving boats, salvage, and general maritime. Business was slow at first, but they started making real money when the recession hit, and desperate vessel owners began sinking their own boats to collect on the insurance. The big property and casualty firms took note of Harris & Chester, Inc., and the partners dove on wrecks from Hoboken to Long Island, providing evidence as to whether the losses were acts of God or acts of Greed.

Their most recent case was a big one, but it was really outside their jurisdiction. Three employees of a waterfront supply outfit in Newark, New Jersey had been murdered in a parking garage in Manhattan. Everybody knew the outfit was Mob-owned, so the NYPD had shrugged at the case. But the families of the dead wouldn't let it lie. They hired Harris & Chester. Four months into the case, the two P.I.'s had plenty of leads, no hard proof, and lots of suspicions.

J.D. Harris and Art Chester figured out pretty quickly that the Newark outfit sold a few anchor chains and wheelhouse instruments but made its real money smuggling cocaine. The waterproof canisters were picked up by air, at night, probably from Colombia, and dumped with a marker not far off St. Barts. One of the faster tourist Cats out of St. Maarten (Harris still didn't know which one) was dropping its load of passengers at the smaller island in the morning, then sailing back out into open water while the tourists shopped and sunned on the beaches. Divers went over the side, picked up the canisters, and affixed them to the insides of the twin hulls. The Cat would then pick up its tourists on St. Barts, head back to Great Bay in St. Maarten, and at night the divers did their work once more.

By collecting rumors and plying loose local lips with whiskey, that was as clear a sketch as Harris and Chester were able to draw. They still didn't know how the coke got to Newark from Great Bay, but they were getting warmer. So warm, in fact, that they'd been warned off by a threatening phone call. But they'd made a lot of enemies in fifteen years in the business, and other such warnings had never scared them off. Arthur Chester was a tough combat veteran and J.D. Harris had quick reflexes and brains. They could handle themselves.

Then they made the big mistake. They got a tip. An anonymous tip. The most dangerous kind. It was a quickly whispered phone call to their New York office, a guy with an Antillean lilt.

There was a sunken wreck of an old British Man'O'War, about half a mile off the southern coast of St. Maarten, in about fifty feet of water. It was a wooden hulled four-master that went down in 1801, so nothing was left but the iron – cannons, portholes, and one huge anchor. The Coke Cat, so the caller claimed, used the wreck for a dead drop. Someplace on the body of that sunken anchor was a small container, and if its contents could be intercepted between the times of the drop and the pickup, all the loose ends would fall neatly into place. It wasn't a stash for drugs, just an information drop, like which plane or boat would be used to make the final run to New York.

Harris and Chester didn't usually bite blind, but this

time they could taste it. Harris didn't want to risk it, but Chester insisted. So, Harris stayed in New York to beat back the work pileup and Arthur Chester went down to St. Maarten to dive on the wreck.

It was a popular dive spot, and to stay inconspicuous, Chester decided to go out there with a group of tourist divers. He had called J.D. the morning of the dive, three days previous, before the weather kicked up.

And then he was gone. He never came back to the boat.

The dive operators had gone crazy looking for him, but with the strong Atlantic currents he might have gone anywhere. There wasn't much hope and for three days the whitecaps made the search impossible.

Diving accidents do happen. Amateurs run out of air and panic, sometimes they cramp up, sometimes a big fish scares them, and they hold their breath and shoot for the surface, blowing their lungs out, and sometimes they just plain drown. But J.D. Harris knew too well that none of those things could have happened to Arthur Chester.

The Renault minibus entered the sprawling resort complex at the Sheraton Mullet Bay. Harris snapped out of his dark thoughts and realized that Jean René Dubois had been talking.

"What'd you say, Jean?"

"I say golf course looks nice and green after few days shower, eh?"

"Yeah. Looks good."

The Sheraton complex was like an island unto itself. The guest houses, restaurants, casinos, and beaches were spread out so far that the customers used courtesy buses to get around.

Jean drove down to the water sports center and dive school. It looked pretty closed up. All lessons and dives had been cancelled due to the weather, and the story of a missing diver probably hadn't helped much. The small concrete dive building huddled near the deserted beach in a grove of high palms. A big red "Diver Down" flag with a white diagonal stripe through the middle whipped in the wind above the roof. The gates were locked up tight.

Dubois parked the Renault in the sand and Harris hauled his equipment to the ground. Dubois got out and stood there staring at the big American. The Antillean's eyes glistened.

"I wait for you here, Meester Harris."

"No, Jean. I don't know how long it'll be."

The black man seemed rooted to the spot. He curled his toes in the sand as if to hang on.

"I think I wait for you."

Harris took him by the arm and guided him back into the driver's seat. He spoke gently.

"Listen, mon ami. I'll be fine. Now go drum up some other business till tonight. You meet me at Epstein's at seven. I'll take care of you then and we'll go out for some food, okay?"

Dubois seemed somewhat appeased, and he forced a gummy smile.

"Okay, boss." He started the engine.

"And Jean," Harris added as if in afterthought. "You need some cash, tell Willie at the desk I said to let you into my room. There's a few bucks in the toe of the left boat shoe in the closet."

He didn't want to say, *If I'm dead you can have the five hundred bucks in my room*, but Dubois' lip turned down at the implication anyway. The Antillean pulled on his sunglasses, said, "Bon chance, mon frère," and drove away.

It was not J.D. Harris' first trip to St. Maarten. He and Chester had been to the Friendly Island before, mostly to escape the dreary diving in the murky waters of New England and rest their eyes on the girls in bikinis. They had come to know the owner of the dive shop at Mullet Bay, a Vietnam vet named Chick O'Connor, who had a shrapnel-scarred body and a nice life in the Caribbean. They liked O'Connor's quiet demeanor and trusted his professionalism, which was why Chester had used Chick's excursion as cover for his dive on the dead drop.

But Harris felt bad about having used O'Connor this way without clueing him in beforehand. As Chick now appeared in his pickup, it was clear he felt even worse for having been unable to save Arthur Chester. He parked the truck in the sand, his shoulders bent as he descended from the cab. God knew he had enough corpses in his past and hadn't needed this one too.

Harris and O'Connor exchanged handshakes and grunted greetings.

"J.D."

"Chick."

The muscular dive master scratched his blond beard and looked at his bare brown feet.

"I lost him, J.D. I lost Chester."

Harris poked a hard finger into O'Connor's chest and left it there.

"You didn't lose shit, O'Connor. I lost him."

They looked at each other for a moment and Harris said, "Gimme a weight belt and twelve pounds and let's go."

They put the gear in the truck and drove over to Simpson Bay Lagoon, where O'Connor had a 24-foot Renegade dive boat gassed up and ready to go. Harris had called Chick the day before and they'd set up the dive for 9:30 am. They hadn't said much on the phone, and now they both knew that each was only angry at himself and no one else. But still there was an edge on it.

Even in the Lagoon the wind had whipped up a pretty good chop and the air tanks banged in the racks at the back of the boat. The two men stood behind the windscreen and squinted with the intermittent sun. Finally, O'Connor spoke. He had to yell above the engine and the wash.

"I wish Chester'd cut me in on it. Then I coulda watched him."

"Yeah. I wish somebody'd watched him." Harris regretted that quickly. "Well fuck me, Chick, and my piss poor mouth."

"Forget it." O'Connor said nothing else for a minute, then he continued. "I don't let nobody dive without a buddy. That's why I've got a good business. Arthur had a buddy, but I guess his buddy was no damn good."

Harris was pulled from his brooding by this new information.

"What buddy? Who was he?"

"Not he, pal. She. Just some tourist on her first open-water. Good lookin' girl. Redhead. Boat was all tourists that day except for Art. I didn't know he needed any protection, so I paired them up. I still don't know shit." O'Connor looked at Harris. "Did he need protection, J.D.?"

"Yeah, he needed it."

"Shoulda known. I never did figure Art for a drowner."

They cut under a low bridge through the channel into Simpson Bay proper and out toward open water where right away the swells grew into whitecaps and troughs. Harris had to hang on hard to the rim of the bridge as the boat danced on the peaks and smashed down into the valleys. They were both soaking wet.

"So, who was this ditsy broad?" asked Harris. He really had to shout now.

"I dunno. Actually, I didn't pair them up. She did. She seemed to take a liking to Art."

Harris' mind churned, along with his stomach. Years in the business had made him a very suspicious man. A "buddy" to a SCUBA diver meant much more than some other kid with you in the pool at summer camp. A SCUBA buddy was supposed to watch your every move, get you out of trouble, save your life if he had to. Or in this case, if she had to. But a first-time diver wouldn't have known what to do in a real emergency. The sight of her buddy drowning would have sent her to the surface in a panic.

O'Connor was shouting again.

"Ya know, these fucking resort courses are for shit, but we do the best we can. Three hours instruction and a little beach diving one day, and then an easy open water dive another day. That's how we make our money. We do it nice and easy and folks get hooked, and then they wanna take the full course, ya know?"

The boat was really crashing now as they rounded the point near Billy Folly and headed straight out toward the wreck site.

"Take is easy," Harris shouted. "I'm a puker."

"It's bad slow, and it's bad fast," said O'Connor. "You wanna get out there and get in the water or ya wanna wallow for a while?"

"Okay. Step on it." Harris clenched his teeth and O'Connor put it at full throttle and it was actually better because the Renegade flew over the waves.

"Tell me more," Harris yelled. "The girl and the dive."

"Well, this broad was slick. She took the resort course last week and picked it up real nice. Ya know how lotsa folks panic the first time under with a tank? Not this girl. Couple a guys couldn't hack it in the rough water off the beach, but she hung in there. Real gutsy."

The sun was out, and the clouds were gone, but Harris left his T-shirt on because his New York skin would burn real fast in the Caribbean heat. O'Connor's scarred body was brown as a pipe bowl. The winds and waves did not diminish.

"So, the other day," O'Connor went on, "she shows up for the dive and so did Art. They were the last ones over the side, and they stayed at the back of the group. We did the usual tour of the wreck. You know, feed the fish, take pictures, all that crap. Art was a pro, didn't use up much air, and she had typical girl's lungs, so all the rest ran out of air first and I took 'em back up. Didn't figure Art much needed me to babysit so I let the two of 'em stay under."

Harris was gripping the bridge rail and trying to focus on one spot on the horizon, but he was hearing every word and picturing it.

"Few minutes later, she pops up all panicky like. Can't find her buddy. So I went over with a fresh tank, looked in every hole I know, and Christ I know every hole down there. Nothin'. When I came back up everybody was real shaky and the girl was sittin' in the boat cryin'. Then I called it in on the radio."

"Ya know," O'Connor added, "Chester ain't the first diver lost in these waters. Last year Spit Williams – guy runs a dive shop on the French side – had a tourist drown and he got swept out to sea in five minutes flat."

Harris still said nothing. O'Connor looked at him hard.

"Was this some hairy operation, J.D.? You ain't told me nothin' yet."

"Yeah, Chick. It's bad news now."

"You're gonna have to tell me a story later."

"I will."

Something had ahold of J.D.'s heart, surrounding it like a fist, squeezing. He didn't want to jump to conclusions, but he was a man who played his hunches, and they were usually on the money. O'Connor watched J.D. just staring out ahead.

"You're thinkin' what I just got myself to thinkin', ain't ya," he said.

"Let's just get down there, Chick."

O'Connor found his spot by quick triangulation from points on shore. He cut the engine, dropped a bow anchor and the now silent boat pitched, yawed, and rolled in the swell. They had their gear on and were in the water in less than a minute.

The transition from waves, wind, and gravity to the silent weightlessness of the undersea had always been a joy to J.D. Harris, but now he didn't care for it. He hadn't been down for a few months and today he'd shaved off his moustache to get a tight mask fit. The rubber irritated the raw skin, but he hardly noticed. He hovered below the white hull for moment, checked the pull on his regulator and his air pressure gauge, and felt for his buckles and straps to ensure all was in order. He glanced at the knife strapped to his leg. He had taken it from the boat.

O'Connor was already out front and below, leading the way, a stream of bubbles rising from his head. The dive master held a 450 triple-sling spear gun in both hands, like he was carrying his M-16 through the jungles of Nam. Ordinarily he would never carry the weapon on a pleasure dive, but he didn't need Harris to tell him to take insurance.

They did not 'descend into the gloom'. The light was strong and the water color was sapphire with a hundred-foot visibility. The sea floor was sixty feet below and the water was only slightly darker there. Big yellowtails, used to being fed scraps of bread by the tourists, crowded around Harris, but he moved through them and followed O'Connor's black swim fins. Large outcroppings of coral reef appeared. Brightly striped clownfish darted in and out of the cattail fans and big blue parrotfish with sharp beaks cruised in pairs. A reed thin trumpetfish poked at some purple fan coral with its mouthpiece and a large stingray fluttered along the sandy bottom. It was like a rich man's aquarium, but today Harris didn't care.

The first sign of the wreck appeared on the shelf of a reef. It was a large cannon, encrusted with rust and coral. J.D. hung there for a moment and equalized the pressure in his ears, pinching his nostrils through the dents in his mask and forcing air into his eustachian tubes. His ears popped and the discomfort was gone.

O'Connor doubled back to him and made a palm-up gesture. What now?

Harris took the lead. Past the cannon, a pair of high coral reefs formed a long winding canyon, and he kicked slowly over a trail of encrusted wreckage – more cannons, the irons of a hatchway, a heavy chain, a porthole. His breathing was slow and steady until he saw the ancient anchor and suddenly his pulse quickened and the air from his tank came in quicker rasps. He rolled onto his back and spotted O'Connor above him, gripping the spear gun and turning his head from side to side like a fighter pilot. O'Connor looked down and gave him the "OK" sign.

Harris slowed his breathing and carried on. The

anchor was a giant, upside down, its rusty shaft the length of half a telephone pole and the curved cross-spar at the top end about twelve feet long, point-to-point. It was in deep shadow, leaning against a coral cliff, like a "T" that had toppled over. The anchor's ring at the bottom of the "T" was buried in the sand and one blade of the cross-spar jutted towards the surface.

Harris exhaled a long breath, letting his weight belt take him down. A small cloud of black and yellow angels burst open and flitted away from the iron monster. He began at the buried end of the shaft, touching nothing, just looking. Even if the story about the dead drop was a phony lead, he figured the site might be rigged somehow to take him out too. But except for the barnacles and rust blisters, the shaft looked clean, and he rose along its angled length for fifteen feet, finding nothing.

Where the shaft intersected with the cross-spar, the underside was in deep shadow. There was a dark smudge where the heavy irons joined, and smaller fish seemed to be feeding on something. He swam in closer, but he still couldn't see what they were pulling at. He reached out a hand and waved them away.

His eyes bugged and he grunted into his regulator, and he back-peddled so hard that his tank clanged against a reef. Salt from his tear ducts stung his eyes and he sank to the seabed and just sat there, his heart pounding against his chest straps and the air from his tank tasting like kerosene. He looked up through his spew of bubbles and saw O'Connor swimming toward him. He waved him off. He forced himself back to the spot.

For a long minute, Harris just stared and blinked. There on the underside of the anchor shaft, a green metallic cylinder was arc-welded to the iron. Just inside its mouth was a small animal trap, of the type used to decapitate rabbits and badgers. The trap had been sprung, its steel teeth like a set of grinning dentures. Clenched between them were two human fingers.

They were white, almost translucent with the effects of the sea water and they'd been nipped at and torn by the feeding fish. Harris tasted bile. He was going to vomit into his regulator. He had heard of many a diver who'd drowned that way after diving seasick off wave-tossed boats, and only his fear of it kept his stomach in check. If he lost it, O'Connor wouldn't be able to save him.

It was only his rage that gave him the strength to do what he had to do next. With his hands shaking, he pulled the knife from his leg scabbard and pried open the steel teeth. The two white digits floated down to the sand. He pulled the knife out and the spring clanged, and he dropped down to the sea floor. No one had to tell him whose fingers lay at his feet, yet something glinted near one of the white knuckles.

It was Arthur Chester's high school football ring.

Harris screamed into his mouthpiece as he lunged at the fingers, scooped them up and shot for the surface. He rocketed past O'Connor, who was shocked into action and swam after him at full tilt, exhaling hard from his lungs. Harris raced for the Renegade's anchor line and spotted the slamming hull above, and he didn't stop howling until he broke the surface, spit out his regulator, grabbed the rim of the boat with his free hand and hurled what was left of his partner into the bridge.

O'Connor burst up beside him like a porpoise, tearing his mask off his face and spitting out his regulator.

"What the fuck, J.D.!"

"Get in the boat, Chick," Harris rasped.

"Did you exhale for Christ's sake? You coulda blown a lung!"

"Just get in the goddamn boat and take my tank."

O'Connor pulled off his own tank and heaved it into the Renegade. He scrambled up the aluminum ladder and reached back to take J.D.'s tank and his weight belt.

Harris clung to a guy rope on the hull. The waves tossed the boat, and the hull banged his head and he gasped for air.

"Chick," he grunted. "Pull anchor and rev her up."

O'Connor moved fast inside the boat. He pulled up the anchor and started the engine, and for a moment he looked down at the deck and froze behind the wheel and hissed, "Mother fuckers."

Harris let the waves bounce him around. He didn't want to get into the boat. He felt it coming, waves of nausea roiling up from deep in his guts and he vomited into the water, over and over, retching hard as the brown cloud spread around him and was quickly taken away by the current. When it was gone, he let the cold seawater wash over his head and sluice through his mouth until he felt clean again.

He hauled himself up the ladder, pulled it over the side and let it bang down on the deck. He collapsed on his back and looked at the rolling sky as O'Connor opened up the throttles, swung about, and headed for home.

"How'd she pay, Chrissy?"

"Cash."

O'Connor and Harris stood outside the dive shack, talking to O'Connor's office manager and long-time dive buddy, a friendly and capable woman long ago from San Francisco. They were doing everything they could to jog their memories about the day of Arthur Chester's "accident".

The sun was full up and the day was already hot despite the stiff breeze, but J.D. Harris stood there shivering in his wet T-shirt and swim trunks. The circular bar on the beach front had just raised its shutters for the day, and O'Connor's other assistant, a native named Tony, appeared with a plastic tumbler full of Jack Daniel's. He handed it to J.D., who thanked him with a nod and tossed back the liquid fire in one gulp. Harris scraped off his T-shirt and tossed it onto the hood of the pickup, which was parked in the sun.

Chrissy held the daily log open in her palms. It was a large loose-leaf with the dive manifests and the medical questionnaires and waivers that would-be divers had to fill out, date, and sign. Her long blond hair brushed the pages as she ran a short fingernail over the listings for the date of the fatal dive.

"Yup, this's gotta be her, 'cause the only other girl that day was dark and had this Italian name here, Guliano."

"Lemme see." O'Connor took the notebook and Harris and Tony looked over his shoulder. "Veronica Barber."

"Yeah, that's right," said Chrissy. "'Cause she called herself Ronnie."

O'Connor looked at the waiver where she'd given her local and home addresses. "La Samana. That's the ritzy hotel just over the French side near Long Beach. Gave her address in the States as 620 East 84th Street in Manhattan."

No one spoke for a moment, and then Harris said, "Cute. Real sweet girl."

"What do you mean?" asked Chrissy.

"There is no 620 East 84th Street in Manhattan." Harris was looking up at the Diver Down flag where it rippled and snapped in the wind. "Unless she lives under the East River."

"Chick, I think maybe we should call in the police, man," said Tony.

"Yeah, maybe we should," Chrissy agreed.

"No." Harris was quick to it. "No cops."

"Why not, Mr. Harris?" asked Tony.

O'Connor did not ask why not.

"'Cause we only have suspicions, Tony," Harris said. "No corpse equals no foul play." Harris caught O'Connor's eye and gave an imperceptible twitch of his head. Chester's fingers were still their secret.

"Anyway," said O'Connor, "You think if this girl did something shitty, she's gonna wait around for the heat?"

"What would you do, Chick?" Harris asked.

Ménage à Noir

Tony jumped in. "I would be long away, Mr. Harris. I would be far away and very fast."

Harris was still looking at O'Connor. "Chick?"

The dive master scratched his beard. "That's what anybody would do. Any amateur. But a pro, a real hard ass… she'd stick around."

"That's right." Harris picked up his Camels from the stone ledge where he'd left them before the dive. He lit up. O'Connor turned to Chrissy.

"Call La Samana and give 'em this name. It's probably phony. Bet they never heard of her."

Chrissy disappeared into the shop.

"Tony," said O'Connor, "if anybody shows up for a lesson this afternoon you and Chrissy can take 'em. But only beach work. No boat. Go work over your gear."

Tony wasn't happy, but he nodded and went into the dive shop, leaving his boss and Mr. Harris alone.

"We'll check out the taxi stands at Mullet first," said Harris.

"Right. If anybody saw her, they'll remember," said O'Connor. "She had a knockout body and a nothing bikini."

Chrissy came back out.

"Like you said, Chick, never heard of her. But I just remembered one more thing. When everybody broke up, they all went over to the courtesy bus stop, and she was with them. Even with that downer day I remember, 'cause I was jealous of those tight cheeks. That bus only runs in one direction from our stop, towards Maho."

"That's why I keep you around," said O'Connor.

Steven Hartov 21

O'Connor and Harris didn't have to go very far. They took the truck over to the Maho Beach Hotel and Casino, part of the Mullet Bay complex, where a number of taxi drivers always hung out waiting for fares. On the way, Harris filled O'Connor in on the case. During the return trip aboard the Renegade, he'd been too weak and sick at heart to speak.

O'Connor had been at Mullet Bay for seven years. He knew every driver who worked the resort and probably most drivers on the island. He talked to a cabbie named Georges, gave him the info and they waited while Georges polled the other drivers in their native Antillean patois, a musical mixture of French, Dutch, English, and local vocabulary. Almost immediately Georges returned with another cab driver, a little man with short white curls on his walnut brown scalp.

"Yes, yes Mr. O'Connor, I remember her." The other driver grinned and almost danced from foot to foot. "She was beautiful girl, long red hair like beak of the Sugar Thief bird. But no, I did not take her to La Samana. She want to go to Little Bay. I remember that was day it rained all afternoon and blowed all night. She did not speak much but very, very pretty."

"Thanks, Hector." O'Connor grabbed the little man's shoulders. "I owe you a drink."

Harris and O'Connor quick-marched to the truck. Harris' nostrils were flaring like a bull's.

"Don't get yourself all worked up," said O'Connor as he started up the truck. "Eighty-twenty the girl's long gone."

"You don't know these people, Chick. They wasted three wharf rats in Manhattan. Eighty-twenty this broad's sunning herself on the beach."

They pulled the pickup onto the main thoroughfare of the Mullet complex and Harris told O'Connor to stop the truck.

"Wait a minute. You got a piece, or maybe a powerhead?"

O'Connor looked at Harris and cut the engine.

"Now look, pal. You calm yourself. What ya gonna do, waste this broad and drag me under with ya?"

"No, I'm not gonna waste her. But we don't know what she's got, or if she's alone. You wanna go naked?"

O'Connor thought for a moment. Then he sighed, started the engine, mumbled, "I thought I was done with all this shit," and headed back for the dive shop.

A powerhead is a special anti-shark device. Mechanically, it's simple. A short gun barrel fits inside a metal sleeve where it can slide freely, and the barrel chambers either a shotgun shell or a large-caliber round. There is a fixed firing pin at the base of the sleeve and the whole mechanism is affixed to the end of a long metal pole.

If a shark approaches within striking distance, the diver yanks a safety pin from the sleeve and drives the end of the barrel against the shark's head, slamming the base of the shell against the firing pin. The shell fires and kills the shark instantly.

Harris and O'Connor drove over the mountains back

towards Philipsburg. They both smoked. Harris held a long canvas gear bag on his lap. The three-foot shaft of the powerhead almost fit into the bag, but the end of the handle with its black plastic bicycle grip poked out through the zipper.

Instead of going into Philipsburg proper they followed Long Wall Road to the head of town, ran down Kerkhof Strat and turned right at Little Bay Road, heading south toward the Little Bay Beach Hotel. They topped a hill, where to the left all of Great Bay and its colorful boats lay spread out under the afternoon sun. Below and to the right, the Little Bay resort lay under rows of palms encircling a secluded beach. It was a special little spot, popular with honeymooners, combining a pristine beach front with open-air cafes, a small night club, and an old-fashioned casino. It was the perfect place for lovers, but love was the last thing on J.D. Harris' mind.

They parked the truck and O'Connor told Harris to wait for him. He knew most of the folks at Little Bay and they threw him a lot of business, but he wouldn't get much cooperation if his friends got a look at the expression on J.D.'s face.

O'Connor walked into the small lobby of the resort. Young couples, some of them burned crimson from the tropical sun, lounged around low wooden tables and sipped tall Piña Coladas. A beautiful Antillean woman sat behind the tourist information desk, and she smiled broadly when she saw O'Connor. She had gold fillings framing her front teeth and luminous green eyes. O'Connor flirted with her.

"Sylvia, you gorgeous thing."

"Oh, Mr. O'Connor!" She blushed, but with her nut-brown cheeks it wasn't visible.

"Listen, babe, I'm looking for one of my students."

O'Connor began to describe the girl, but he didn't get far.

"Oh, you must be talking about Miss Red. I do not know her last name, but she is very beautiful."

"Yeah, that's her, hon. Red."

"She lives down at the end, a beach room. It is 129, I think. Oh, but I am sorry for you, Mr. O'Connor." Sylvia placed her chin on her palm and raised an eyebrow. "I think she is leaving today."

"Well, maybe I'll catch her. I'll catch you too, but later."

"Oh, you," said Sylvia, but O'Connor was out the door.

Harris and O'Connor walked carefully along the cement boardwalk that led to the beachfront rooms. They scanned the sand and all the lounge chairs and examined the water for a mane of red hair, but no one fit the image of "Red."

They entered a long corridor, arriving at the last of the attached rooms at the farthest end of the resort. The left side of the hallway was walled with latticework and half open to the Atlantic breezes from Great Bay. The beach side was lined with doors. They found room 129.

Harris clutched the gear bag and stood off to the right of the door. O'Connor took the left and pointed to his own chest. Harris nodded. O'Connor rapped a knuckle on the door.

A voice answered, somehow not the voice Harris expected. It was a sweet female voice, drowsy with the sun and the sea.

"Yes? Who is it?"

O'Connor's voice dropped to a syrupy hum, taking on the accent of a native Antillean. Harris raised an eyebrow, impressed.

"Tow-ells, miss. I bring clean tow-ells."

There was a short pause.

"Thanks, but I have towels."

Sweat beaded on O'Connor's forehead. He stared at Harris, who quickly looked around and then rapped his own knuckles on the wooden door.

"Oh, for Christ's sake," they heard her mumble and suddenly the doorknob turned and like twin machines fired by the same electrical charge Harris and O'Connor burst into the room.

The girl jumped back, and O'Connor quickly slammed the door.

Images flashed through Harris' brain. The big glass French doors to the beach were closed and gauzy white curtains filtered the light into a shady gloom. An air conditioner was blowing hard, and the room was cold. The girl was stunning, even with her mouth open in stupid surprise. Her dark red hair was wet and slicked back from her forehead and down her back and her hands had come away from where they held a white coverup closed over her body. Her breasts still held the wrap mostly in place.

A huge dark figure leaped up from the sheets of a rumpled bed and Harris inhaled the musty smell of sex.

O'Connor recognized the naked man. It was Tom-Tom, a pit boss in the Great Bay Casino, known for his toughness and the pleasure he derived from dispatching rowdy customers. Suddenly all of O'Connor's doubts about the girl's culpability flew away. Tom-Tom drove a fancy French sports car and flashed a lot of cash for a casino goon. O'Connor had always wondered where the big man got his money.

Harris was taking in something else, a pile of sophisticated SCUBA gear in one corner of the room. There was a single tank and a double rig, plus an assortment of masks, regulators, and pressure gauges – not the stuff of a beginner.

J.D. Harris was not the polite investigator. He believed that surprise was his element and often the first verbal exchange could reveal a suspect's guilt or innocence. He could read eyes like the FBI read polygraphs. He fought to control his voice.

"I'm the other half, lady."

The redhead just stood there, gaping.

"You watched my partner, didn't ya. Watched his moves, his hotel. Then you followed him out to Mullet and signed up for the dive, your first dive my ass. Buddied up to him. Ol' Art was a sucker for a body like that. He liked women. He also liked his life."

Tom-Tom stood on the other side of the bed. His huge shoulders were bunched, and he was clenching his big fists. He grunted and started moving around the bed. O'Connor put out a palm.

"Now you be cool, Tom-Tom. You just be real cool."

Harris seemed to only see the girl.

"And then what, Red? Or whatever your name is. Art was no fool. He wouldn't have just stuck his hand in that rig, so you shoved his elbow. Got his hand in a real tight jam, didn't he, and then what'd ya do, help him lose his regulator?"

Harris was hissing now through clenched teeth, but the girl had composed herself and managed to speak.

"You're nuts, mister."

"Yeah? And then what? When his lungs were full of seawater and he got nice and quiet, you ripped him free and let the current take him. Right?"

"You're out of your fucking mind," she said.

"Ya think so?" Harris slowly reached into the gear bag and came out with a clenched fist. "Then what's this?"

He opened his hand, quickly, and there in his trembling palm was Arthur Chester's finger with the ruby of his class ring gleaming.

The girl screamed. Tom-Tom scooped up something from the floor and suddenly he had a weight belt with ten pounds of iron arcing over his head. O'Connor yelled and launched himself at Tom-Tom's wrist, but Harris already had the powerhead out and the pin pulled. Harris charged the girl, elbowing her face and knocking her to the bed, and then like an Olympic fencer he lunged at the pit boss, driving forward two-fisted with the powerhead and slamming the barrel into Tom-Tom's thigh bone just above his left knee. The explosion banged in the small room and the big man's legs flew out from under him. He slammed to the floor on his face and squealed like a wounded animal, his hands scrabbling to grip one of the bed legs. There was blood on the wall behind him. The stench of scorched powder filled the room.

O'Connor steadied himself where he'd fallen against a mirrored dresser. The weight belt had shattered the mirror. Harris just stood where he was, breathing. The girl was curled up at one corner of the bed, clutching her robe. But she did not cry. She stared at Harris.

Harris reached into the gear bag and pulled out another shotgun shell. He cleared the barrel of the powerhead and reset the chamber with the fresh shell. O'Connor was staring at him.

"Don't, J.D… Don't."

Then the girl began to plead.

"No, please, my God, I didn't want to do it to him. I had to. I had to. You don't know these people. I had to."

"Don't, J.D." O'Connor was frozen against the dresser. "Jay Dee don't do it."

Harris took another moment to breathe. He had what he wanted, and a witness.

"Lady, you goddamn…" He struggled for the words. "You better hope there's an extradition treaty with the States. 'Cause if there isn't, I'm gonna kill you, right here on this friendly island. Maybe not today, or even this week. But soon. Real soon."

He handed the powerhead to O'Connor, and then he bent and gently picked up Arthur Chester's finger from the floor. He opened his shirt pocket, took out his Camels and buttoned the finger inside. He lit up, but he had a hard time striking the match. He ignored the big man moaning on the floor.

"Watch 'em, Chick," he said to O'Connor. "Watch 'em real good. I'm gonna go outside and throw up. And then I'm gonna call the cops, if they're not already here."

J.D. Harris walked out of the hotel room. He slammed the door behind him as the girl finally started to cry.

Inside, Chick O'Connor gripped the powerhead in both hands. He turned to the two figures in the gloom of the room, and he watched them real good.

2. THE OTHER END OF NEWBURY STREET

FRIEDLAND WAS SITTING in an Irish bar on the corner of Massachusetts Avenue and Newbury Street. It was 1975 and it wasn't the classy end of Newbury. Not the downtown end where F.A.O. Schwartz was almost hidden away, and La Crepe served fancy French blintzes to Ivy League types. It wasn't the section of Newbury where in the spring, students who'd skipped classes lounged at overpriced outdoor cafes, drinking espresso and pretending to be in Paris while discussing Renaissance painters in serious, nasal tones.

It was the other end of Newbury, the part that dissolved around midtown into a grey haze of custom photography shops and cramped, overly crowded music stores. It was the slice of Newbury that bordered Boston's No-Man's Land, intersecting with Mass Ave where the Turnpike sprang out of the city tunnels and started to make noise. Not quite downtown, and not yet uptown with the trees and Brookline and Brighton. It was the crossroads of Boston, where choosing a different direction meant a different life.

The bar was called Doyle's, though only those who frequented the place knew that. There was no sign outside, only the word BAR stamped in green letters on a heavy wooden and glass door. The door was sunk back into the brownstone, as if the proprietor wanted no new members for his club, like a Prohibition speakeasy.

Inside, everything was dark heavy wood. The floor was nearly black with years of scuff marks. It ran the length of the bar and reached back into the small saloon like the abused tarmac of some clandestine South American airstrip. A few booths lined one wall that flanked the back alley. The windows were small and slimy and crisscrossed with wrought iron.

The shelf behind the bar was lined with half-empty booze bottles sporting metal barman's spouts. A large mirror was carelessly mounted over the shelf and the remaining wall space in the place was mostly bare, except for a few old beer hall prints that did nothing for the atmosphere. The largest print was at the far end of the establishment, hung next to a battered door indicating MEN in black peeling letters. The print was of Custer's Last Stand, all tans and yellows. Faded history.

Doyle himself was behind the bar. He was fat, bald, and shiny, and he chomped a spit-soaked cigar that looked like a touch added to the scene by the prop department. He held a dirty white dish towel in his fat right hand and was swirling it around the inside of a shot glass clenched in his left. There was a whole pile of wet shot glasses on the bar. The "clean" ones went back onto the shelf underneath. Bob Dylan moaned "Simple Twist of Fate" from Doyle's juke box.

Friedland was the only other person in the joint. He sat at the last booth along the alley wall, facing the door. He liked to think of his business as dangerous, and so, as men in danger will do, he always sat facing the door. He was hunched over the table, resting on his elbows and staring down into a large whisky tumbler that turned between his stubby fingers. His dark curly hair still glistened with beads of rain that trickled down the outsides of the windows. His steel rimmed glasses were still foggy from the street.

Ever since he'd splurged and had the hook taken out of his nose, Friedland's glasses never seemed to stay all the way on. It just hadn't seemed right for a private investigator to have a hook in his nose. But then the change hadn't brought more clients either. He'd developed a habit of using the little finger of his right hand to push the bridge of his glasses up onto his nose. He did that now and nursed a sip from the whiskey glass. Then he resumed twirling the glass and staring into it as a pattern of thoughts began to swirl, a sort of self-bolstering sermonette that usually preceded any decision Friedland was about to make.

'Now it takes real class,' he thought. 'It takes real class to buy a white trench coat. A guy who really has it don't even think about the color. He don't think about the dirt. He don't think about the city, the rain, the smog, the soot. A guy with class just goes into Saks and picks himself out a nice white trench coat. With lapels. And a silk lining. It's got a collar you can turn up and it stays there, and the body's tapered a little... And this same guy, he don't buckle the belt buckle. He takes the two ends of the belt and ties 'em in a knot. Then he's got real deep pockets to stick his hands in. The sleeves got little straps on 'em too. With buttons.'

Friedland nodded to no one as the amber liquid shimmered in his tumbler.

'Yeah. A guy with real class, he buys himself a white trench coat and he don't even think about the dirt. Gets a little speck on it, bingo, twenty-four-hour dry cleaners. Got an account there 'cause he ain't scared to buy white clothes.'

By this time, a slight smile had stretched between the jowls in Friedland's cheeks. Then he looked down at the frayed hem of the brown car coat hanging lifelessly about his knees. He frowned.

The bar door opened. For a moment the traffic and the rain drowned out Dylan, then it closed again, and a man stepped inside. Friedland stiffened. The guy was tall, broad, with iron gray hair, a cleft chin and a straight nose nobody'd worked on. He wore an expensive suit, pearl sheen tie, and no overcoat, just a James Cagney hat. He shook it off, spotted Friedland, strode the length of the saloon and slipped into the booth facing the private eye. He dropped the wet hat on the table.

"Albert," he said. He had a voice like a lawn mower.

"Mr. White." Friedland nodded. He figured that wasn't the man's real name.

"Show me whatcha got."

Friedland reached into his car coat and pulled out a five-by-seven brown envelope. From that he extracted five black and white photos, glossy finish, and spread them out for Mr. White, along with a crooked smile like they were a royal flush. They'd turned out pretty good considering he'd developed them in his bathtub.

White looked them over, but he didn't touch them. They showed a comely blonde in a tight paisley blouse, short suede skirt and pumps, smiling at a guy half White's age on a street corner somewhere. The younger guy wore a leather jacket, jeans, Frye boots, and had gelled black hair. The other shots showed the couple walking up the steps of a brownstone, with the younger guy grinning and flicking a butt into a potted plant, and then both of them going inside.

White looked up at Friedland. His dark eyes were slitted and stormy.

"These are tourist shots, Albert. Where's the meat?"

Friedland's jowls flushed. "What d'ya mean?"

"I told you I needed shots of them in flagrante delicto."

"Huh?" Friedland cocked his head like a dog.

"I need shots of them banging, Albert. Or at least buck naked."

"How am I supposed to get those?" Friedland's palms turned up and his fading smile trembled.

"I don't know, Albert. You're the private dick. Pick a lock. Climb a tree somewhere."

"But that ain't legal."

White's face flushed. He leaned in. Friedland slunk back.

"Listen, dick, I need to dump this gold digger chick. She's steppin' out on me. But if I don't have the goods on her she'll clean me out. I thought you got that, Albert. I thought I made that clear." White slapped the photos with a meaty hand. "These snaps are friggin' useless."

"I'll try again, Mr. White."

"Forget it." White pushed the photos away. He reached inside his suit and pulled out an alligator wallet. "I told you you'd get half a large if you delivered. Now you get a fin." He pulled out a fifty, slapped it on the booth table, got up and put on his hat.

"And Albert," he said as he burned Friedland's eyes with his own. "Lose my number."

Then he walked away.

Friedland watched him go. The door slammed. He collected up his photos, put the fifty in his car coat, sighed, and for a moment just slumped.

There was a scraping sound as Friedland pushed his glass away from his hands and slid out of the booth. He moved quickly to the bar and pulled a small wad of bills from his trouser pocket. He peeled off a few singles and slapped them down on the wet wood. Doyle didn't even look up.

"See ya later, Jimmy," said Friedland as he trotted for the door.

"See ya, gumshoe," replied Doyle. He said it without humor. He was still wiping the shot glasses.

Friedland was out on Mass Ave and turned left

without faltering. He walked briskly along the sidewalk, his head bowed, and shoulders hunched against the wind and drizzle. He dodged other commuters with small fast boxer's steps and turned left again onto Boylston Street.

He reached the back entrance to the Mass Ave station of the "T" – the main entrance was locked up for repairs – and tiptoed down the stairs into the tunnel. He fished for a quarter and threw it into the metal turnstile and descended another stairway to wait for the Green Line downtown. He tapped a foot on the concrete and waited for the train with his hands in his pockets. He watched his breath cloud in the damp air until a train marked GOV. CENTER came rattling along the tunnel from out of town, then he boarded the ancient car and huddled into a seat.

But Friedland failed to get off at the Prudential stop, where Saks Fifth Avenue had a branch store in the insurance skyscraper. Instead, he continued downtown, and got off wearily at the Government Center stop where he walked slowly over to Filene's Department Store and down into the bargain basement.

He got himself a navy-blue trench coat with lots of grenade rings and extra straps for thirty-five bucks, and he paid for it with Mr. White's fifty, because he knew his own check wouldn't clear.

Friedland wasn't really happy with himself when he left Filene's, but a guy had to be practical. Someday soon he'd get that really big break, a case only he could crack, and it would make all the papers. The lady who'd taken him on would be rich, and when he found her kidnapped kid he'd be set for life. Then he'd buy that white trench coat and never look back.

Out on the street again, the rain was really starting to hammer, but he decided to hoof it all the way back on Newbury and break in his new blue trench. He was still daydreaming about that big case, head down in the rain, when he jaywalked a light and a bus plowed him into a taxi with a sound like a mallet smacking a wet paper bag full of walnuts.

For a while, Jimmy Doyle wondered what had happened to Friedland. But Doyle never read the obituaries, only the betting sheets.

He figured Friedland had moved to Florida.

3. POCKET LITTER

CAPTAIN EYTAN ECKSTEIN sat in a cold metallic chair at Neumann's sidewalk café, just down the block from St. Stephen's Cathedral.

October in Vienna brought the winds from the east, yet the weather had not yet diminished the tourists. They flocked and chattered and overflowed the platz, many in crimson or black cashmere coats, thick furs, scarves, berets, and smart caps. Their dollars and marks and lira made the red-cheeked Austrian shop keepers happy, and even though the chill air was laced with lung steam, hardly a seat remained empty at any establishment.

Eckstein liked it that way. Crowds made for good camouflage.

He looked at his black leather gloves as they gripped the newsprint of the Herald Tribune. The headline trumpeted a tragedy, the fall of a Boeing airliner over Scotland. It was all very fresh, and no one had yet claimed the 'wet work,' as the Russians called it, but he had no doubts about the handprints of terror. One didn't need to be an officer in Israeli Military Intelligence to understand that such things were rarely accidental these days. Yes, commercial aircraft occasionally fell from the sky due to mechanical flukes, but more often than not they were split into flaming debris by high explosives. Many people were dead, including four employees of Israel's Ministry of Defense, and someone in Vienna knew why.

Eckstein glanced down at his grey woolen trousers. He'd begun his career as a paratroop officer, and it still felt strange to be serving in civilian garb. At times he longed for his uniform and the simplicity of combat, good guys and bad all properly costumed. His blue eyes frowned as he flicked off a flake of chocolate croissant, took a sip of the mélange from his round metal table, and looked over the top of the paper. Across the large promenade of gleaming cobblestones and clicking boot soles, he saw Lieutenant Colonel Benjamin Baum just there under the Mont Blanc awning.

Baum's hefty girth was encased in a fir green car coat, a Tyrolean hat with a feather on his balding pate, looking much like his Bavarian ancestors. Linked to his arm was that new girl from Jerusalem HQ, Nava, a pretty little thing on her first job abroad. She was playing Baum's daughter and clearly enjoying the role as she gestured at the glossy black fountain pens inside the store and bounced on her modest brown pumps.

Eckstein watched as Baum stroked her auburn hair, maneuvered himself between her and the windows and raised his meaty hands, as if admonishing her exorbitant tastes. Yet with his back to the glass now, Baum looked over her scalp and his eyes met Eckstein's. The colonel cocked his head just a bit to his right. They were coming.

Eckstein shifted his gaze to the left. There, just astride a multi-canopied Schnitzelhaus, a throng of schoolgirls were skipping away, as between them his contacts waded forward between the bobbing pigtailed heads. There were three of them, not two as arranged, but with his cover as a British journalist he could hardly object. The one out front was certainly Nidal, a rough bit player and remnant of Black September. He was small and wiry in a black leather jacket, with a reputation for favoring profit over politics. The two behind were muscle, wearing long woolen coats, scarves, and scowls. All of them had black curly hair and their dark eyes hunted for Eckstein and nothing else. They looked like jackals in a kindergarten.

He signaled Benni Baum with a touch to one nostril, folded the paper and glanced at the white rose on his table. The flower was a bit melodramatic, but that's what they'd asked for. Normally such a meet would be the purview of the civilian Mossad, but Military Intelligence—acronym AMAN—had developed Nidal from a false-flag missile buyback in Khartoum. First come, first served, gentlemen. Our spy, not yours. It was always that way.

Nidal slowed as he approached Eckstein's perch. His eyes were shrouded in photo-grey glasses, and he had a small pink scar on his clean-shaven chin. No one had actually seen him before, so this in itself was a coup, and Eckstein imagined his teammate Yaakov snapping away with a long lens from somewhere. Nidal looked down at the rose, then scanned the area beyond Eckstein's head, pulled out a chair and sat to his right. Eckstein palmed his own chair arms, raised his buttocks, and sat back down. He thought it a strange greeting, rather like releasing gas, yet it was oh-so British.

"Mr. Hearthstone," said Nidal with a nod. He had a voice like Lebanese honey mixed with gravel.

"Anthony, if you please," Eckstein said in his London lilt.

With that much affirmed, the two heavies pulled out chairs and sat to Eckstein's left. From that point on they appeared uninterested in the conversation, chatted in Algerian French, and ogled the Austrian girls. Nidal reached into his leather jacket, while Eckstein struggled to avoid watching his fingers. Not long ago in Madrid, an agent had been killed exactly this way, right off the top of the meet. But Nidal came up with a silver cigarette case, flicked it open and offered Eckstein a smoke. The case was filled with slim black sticks.

"Thanks awfully," Eckstein said with a smile. "But I'm doing my best to quit. And those are Balkan Sobranies, much too strong I'm afraid."

"As you wish." Nidal produced a gold rimmed lighter and lit up. "But you will never be able to quit here in Europe. Perhaps only in America, where they all pretend to hate their vices."

Eckstein smirked. "That's why the Colonies aren't my favorite."

A waitress appeared. She was blonde with strudel braids, a white bodice and creamy cleavage. The heavies looked up and grinned.

"Getränke, meine Herren?" she asked.

"Noch nicht, danke," said Nidal. His German was smooth.

She dipped a curtsy and swayed away. Nidal leaned back and exhaled a blue cloud.

"So, Mr. Hearthstone. Pierre said you work for the Telegraph."

Pierre Dumont was a cutout in Nice, a pay-for-play neutral working all sides. Such men were the pilot fish of the intelligence trade.

"Yes," said Eckstein, "amongst other publications."

AMAN had a 'helper' at the Telegraph in London, a nice Jewish lady with a daughter serving in the Israeli Army. If queried, she'd confirm Anthony Hearthstone as a stringer, and she even penned articles under his name and arranged for payments to his Barclays account. The use of the internet was just beginning to surge, and someday soon it would become a spy's nemesis, with all such details too easy to check. But for now, his cover would hold. Eckstein made sure to read everything 'he' published. Some of it was quite good.

"Of course," said Nidal. "One should never depend on a single employer. And where are you from in England?"

"Southampton, a rather oily town with a quay and too many sailors."

"I know that city," said Nidal as he watched Eckstein's eyes. "I have been there."

Eckstein wasn't concerned. He never referenced a place in which he hadn't spent considerable time.

"My condolences," he said. "I fled to London in the

spring of my youth." He glanced over at the two heavies, who were heads-down examining the advertising card of an escort service and commenting lewdly in French. "So, shall we discuss the subject at hand?"

He reached into his coat for a small notebook and pen. The heavies glanced up, but he ignored them. He hadn't his pistol or even a small blade, which made him feel terribly naked. But if he were armed and they decided to frisk him, it would all end right there.

"You will not need notes," said Nidal. "We agreed only upon a photograph and a name."

"Quite right, my good man. Just a lead." Eckstein nodded and put the notebook away. "A photo and a name, which will hopefully lead me to other such names."

Nidal pulled another long drag from his Sobranie and streamed the smoke from his nostrils.

"In return for which?" he posed.

"Two thousand thanks from the Crown."

Nidal raised an eyebrow. "That is quite a substantial sum, Mr. Hearthstone."

"Well." Eckstein tapped the Herald. "My employers think this might be the scoop of my career."

"Perhaps but pursuing it might also prove dangerous. This man whose name I shall give you is not so friendly as me."

"Have no fear, Nidal. I never reveal a source. It's bad for business."

"It would not matter if you did." The informant smiled, yet the expression did not touch his eyes. "Since Nidal is not really my name."

Eckstein's eyes crinkled. "Can't say I'm shocked."

"Is Hearthstone really yours?"

"Given on the day of my Baptism." Eckstein feigned a wounded expression. "Haven't you read my bylines?"

"Of course."

Then Nidal did something strange. He twirled the cigarette from his first two fingers to his pinky, then back again, and popped it back in his lips. Eckstein noted the inadvertent clue: the man was a practiced card player or amateur magician.

"So then," said Nidal, "any personal theories so far?"

"Well." Eckstein tapped his lips, then brushed a lock of his blondish hair back from his brow. "My first thoughts ran to the Iranians, due to that messy cock-up in the Gulf. However, Ahmed Jabril's my runner up."

"Educated guesses, though you might be off-target. Think Libya."

"You don't say?" Eckstein tilted his chin. "That one hadn't crossed my mind."

"Colonels who become kings have long memories, especially once they've been bombed by the west."

"Quite. And this fellow whose name you shall give me. Would he happen to be a resident of Tripoli?"

"I suppose you'll find out. Do you have a business card?"

Eckstein reached into his coat, produced a mahogany Marks & Spencer wallet, and slipped out a card. He passed it across the table and Nidal picked it up and ran his manicured fingers over the relief.

"Not to be impolite," Eckstein said, "but do you have something for me in return?"

Nidal reached inside his leathers and plucked out a small envelope. Eckstein's pulse surged. They were getting close, but he showed the man nothing, and he didn't dare let his eyes search for Benni or the rest of the team. There were eight of them as backup, mobile, well-armed and quick, and he simply had to trust they were out there somewhere and ready for whatever might happen next.

Nidal twirled the envelope as if it were an Ace of Spades. He said, "Now I'd like to see something a bit fatter than this."

Eckstein opened his coat. Inside, poking up from the left–hand pocket, was a hefty bank envelope.

"Ahh, we're almost there," said Nidal. Then he tucked his own envelope away and stretched out his brown hand, palm up. But he didn't ask for the money. "May I have your wallet, please?"

Eckstein blinked. "Excuse me?"

"Your wallet, Mr. Hearthstone." Nidal was no longer smiling, and the two heavies were leaning in now, staring at Eckstein's eyes.

Hoo mikzo-ee mizdayen, Eckstein thought in Hebrew. He's a fucking professional. Probably trained at Patrice LaMumba.

"Well, I suppose, if you wish," he protested weakly. "But it's certainly not the norm, my good man."

"In my line of work, there is no norm." Nidal's upturned fingertips twitched.

Eckstein sighed, plucked out his wallet again and

handed it over. He would have to play this carefully: offended, but not alarmed. He folded his arms in a casual huff and looked away, watching the passing crowd.

In fact, he was barely perturbed. Some years ago, at the beginning of his career with AMAN, the tools of tradecraft had been hammered into his brain as if it were a molten sword on an anvil. Benni Baum himself had supervised the courses, which more than anything else, emphasized cover. Eckstein could still hear Benni's rough Bavarian accent.

"Always assume that you are going to be captured and stripped. Not a single clothing label should be Israeli, nor your pens, pencils, coins, shoes, or socks. And an innocent civilian is always a walking waste basket. He has receipts from the laundry, notes from his wife, and his wallet is stuffed with the things of his life. You will find a constantly updated selection with the quartermaster but choose things that make sense and that you know well. We will supply your passports, driving licenses, credit cards and the like, all with your own photographs and signatures. However, the rest of it should match your own tastes and habits. We call it all 'pocket litter,' but it is the gold bullion of your survival."

Eckstein listened to the rustle of Nidal's fingers flipping through his imposter life. Everything in there was up to date, British credit cards, British license, photos of the family of one of the analysts who he knew well enough to pretend were his own. Most of the rest was from London: receipts from pubs, bookstores, and petrol stations. There were also a few from Vienna, because without them he'd appear to have dropped from the sky.

He looked back at Nidal as the rustling stopped. Nidal was holding up a single green ticket, a stub from the film noir classic, "The Third Man". Ever since the film's release in 1948 it had been playing regularly at Vienna's Burg Kino cinema on Opernring. Just two months before while passing through Austria, Eckstein had caught a showing again. The tickets were convenient because they displayed no date.

"I like this film," said Nidal as he twirled the ticket between his thumb and finger.

"Well, you're a man of good tastes."

"The performances are so true to life. Orson Welles and William Holden, yes?"

"Welles and Joseph Cotton, actually," Eckstein corrected.

"Of course. When did you last see it?"

"Night before last, in fact."

Nidal nodded and carefully replaced all of the receipts into Eckstein's wallet. He handed it back and Eckstein put it away and glanced at his watch.

"Shall we proceed?" he suggested impatiently. "I do have another appointment."

"Yes. The Sterlings, if you please."

Eckstein pulled out the bank envelope and placed it on the Herald, with his gloved fingers holding it in place. But Nidal didn't produce his envelope in kind. Instead, he set his elbows on the table, laced his fingers together, leaned in and spoke in nearly a whisper.

"You did not see 'The Third Man' the night before last, Mr. Hearthstone. The Burg Kino is closed for renovations."

Eckstein felt a flush of heat rushing up through his chest. But his training kicked in and he cooled his quickening pulse and cocked his head.

"Well, perhaps I made a mistake," he offered. "Might have actually been last week."

Nidal tipped his glasses up away from his eyes. They were burning like coals in a hearth and his lips curled back from his teeth.

"The cinema's been closed for a month." He dragged the bank envelope from Eckstein's fingers, stuffed it into his jacket and zipped it up. "I think perhaps we should take a walk," and he added with a sneer, "my good man."

Ya'allah, ayzeh fashlah! My God what a fuckup! It flashed through Eckstein's brain and his heart succumbed to the adrenaline and started hammering in his chest. The game was up and there was no way to recover it now. For a second he thought about bolting, but then he glanced at the two heavies, who were staring at him as if he were a freshly skinned lamb on the eve of Eid Al-Fitr. The left one had opened his coat, and his fingers were close to the butt of a holstered handgun. If Eckstein leapt up and sprinted, he might make it for a few meters, but these men would gun him down in the back, right there in the square. He breathed out a long, ragged sigh.

"I suppose it's a good day for a stroll, given the weather."

In a moment the three had risen and surrounded him in a wedge. He slid his chair back and got up, intentionally 'forgetting' to leave cash for his fare and hoping the waitress would come charging after them. He'd need only that small distraction to hurl one of them into the others and flee. But Nidal was no fool and he dropped some crumpled bills on the table and took Eckstein's elbow and walked, with the heavies so close on their heels that Eckstein could smell their cologne.

He heard Benni Baum's admonitions booming inside his head. "Never leave the primary location unless there is no other choice. If you do, and you fail to signal all's well, we'll assume you are under duress."

Well, I am fucking under duress, Eckstein thought. And you won't get a signal from me unless they jam a finger up my ass.

He kept his hands tightly along his trouser seams and felt Nidal's threatening grip. Maybe it would turn out all right, he thought. Maybe they'd just march him along, curse his duplicity, relish in blowing his cover, then take off with the money and leave him red-faced and empty-handed. Wouldn't that make the most sense for Nidal? An easy payday? No blood, no foul?

But then it got worse. Nidal, instead of walking along the promenade where the crowds would provide ample cover for the team to follow, turned and strode directly across the cobblestone expanse, heading for St. Peter's Church. It was a huge old edifice with an enormous green dome, yet it wasn't a prime tourist attraction, and it was only busy on Sunday Mass. But this wasn't a Sunday, and its stone stairs and circular base were empty, and Eckstein knew that behind the church were warrens and alleyways crawling away into dark urban labyrinths.

"Now the truth, Mr. Hearthstone," Nidal hissed. "Who are your employers?"

"The Telegraph, as I told you."

Always deny, until you can deny no more, and then lie and lie well.

"Reporters are whores, but they lie about big things. You've made a fatal error and lied small."

"Oh, for heaven's sake, Nidal," Eckstein scoffed. "Just call them up. You've got my card and the telephone number. There's a bank of telephones right back in the square."

Protest, stretch it out, give the team as much time as you possibly can.

"I have no doubt that even the Prime Minister would lie for you, Hearthstone. The question is, which one?"

"This is outrageous!" Eckstein stopped in his tracks, threw up his hands and raised his voice. "You've been generously compensated, and I expect to be as well, Nidal."

As a last resort make a scene, because once they've got you somewhere else, we'll never reach you in time.

Nidal gripped Eckstein's bicep, higher and tighter, and pushed his face so close that a fleck of spittle struck Eckstein's cheek. "I despise melodrama," he said. "It always makes me want to end the performance."

Eckstein felt something metal jolt his spine, and they walked again, past the rear of the church now and heading for slimmer and darker, empty streets. He glanced up at a cluster of low hanging clouds and felt the first spittle of evening drizzle. The tourist bustle behind them had faded into murmurs and the weak violin strains of a street musician, leaving only the clicks of their shoes on slick stones.

When you finally give something up, make it good and make it stick.

"All right, all right," said Eckstein. "It shouldn't fucking matter to you at all since you're here for a payday, but I'm bloody MI6."

"British Intelligence. That is very convenient," said Nidal. "But too quick. If you'd said that at our next stop, with my comrades here breaking your thumbs, I might have believed it."

He was right and Eckstein knew it and cursed himself, but he'd been pistol whipped before and just wasn't up for it. One of the heavies behind him laughed.

"Well, what the hell did you expect?" Eckstein protested. "It was a plane full of Brits falling on a village full of Scots. Who else would be interested in this thing?"

Instantly he knew that last part was a mistake.

Always think like a trial attorney. Never ask a leading question that might open you up.

"Since you asked," said Nidal. "I think you might be working for Jerusalem."

Eckstein felt weak in the knees.

"Bollocks!" he sputtered and forced a mocking laugh. "The bloody Jews?"

"Yes." Nidal began to trot along faster, and Eckstein had to stretch his pace to keep up. "I think my guess is good, and we're going to find out. In fact, in exchange for one of your fingers, I might be compensated doubly by persons more generous than you, or the Telegraph, or MI6."

Koos em-mek, Eckstein cursed silently in Arabic. Your mother's twat. His vision was narrowing, his breathing labored, a pulse in his neck pounding twice for each second.

It was growing darker and wetter, and they were now moving along a slim alleyway with cement-faced apartments above and bed sheets dangling from drooping lines. At the end, about a hundred meters on, he saw the curved façade of a closed laundromat and his bowels clenched. Was that the bastards' safe house? Turn on the washing machines and no one can hear you scream? He heard a set of keys jangling behind him. He thought he could see an exit from the end of the alley to the right, but he wasn't sure. In a moment he'd be there inside and gone from the world.

He knew he could kill Nidal with a knife-hand blow to his throat, and maybe he'd take down one of the heavies. But he couldn't get to all three of them before a bullet punched through his sternum. Dying like this, for God's sake, in Vienna no less. Just another Jew sprawled out on the streets of Hitler's favorite city. His mother would spin in her grave. Where the hell are you, Baum?

He heard the motorcycles before he saw them. Not an urgent sound of racing engines, but an easy rumbling echo through the alleyway walls. The gleaming fenders of two green Ducati's coasted in at the end of the alley, but Nidal and his thugs hesitated only briefly, because the sounds of female laughter accompanied the bikes. Then the throaty machines appeared from around the corner, side by side, each with a helmeted male driver in front, both of them hugged by comely girls from the back. The girls had no helmets, a blonde and a redhead, lip-sticked and laughing and the bikes were so close together that one of them tweaked the other's cheek. The riders coasted slowly toward Eckstein and his captors, cheery and chatting, a quartet of lovers out for some vibrating foreplay.

Eckstein slowed. Nidal gripped him harder and dragged him. A fist punched his spine from behind. He watched the motorcycles coming on, a bit faster now, the drivers dipping their heads. He saw the blonde on the right pass something gleaming to the redhead on the left, then the laughter ended abruptly, and the engines roared, and it was as if they'd been launched from the flight deck of a carrier, and they went from zero to sixty in a gut-pounding second. He felt Nidal stiffen, and he saw the bikes split and then he saw the heavy chain stretched taut between the fists of the girls at neck height.

He dove flat to his face on the slick cold stones as the engines deafened him and the black wheels thundered by, and he heard half a muffled scream and the crack of metal against bone, and skull against skull, and in an instant, he was up on his feet again.

The motorcycles were gone, leaving nothing but trails of blue smoke. Nidal was splayed on his back, his glasses gone and a wild rent across his face that had taken part of his nose. One of the heavies was flat on his face in the other direction, his limp hands by his sides and turned up. The other one, who'd been jabbing Eckstein with his handgun, sat on his rump like a confused toddler, holding his bloody scalp with one hand as he fumbled for the fallen pistol between his trembling knees.

Eckstein took two quick strides, cocked his right leg back and round-housed the heavy in the chin with his shoe. The man toppled back, and his head bounced on stone. Eckstein kicked the pistol away as he heard a female voice from above yell, "Was ist loss hier?" He ignored her and jumped back to Nidal and fumbled madly inside his jacket until he came up with the small envelope and took off, sprinting back towards St. Peter's. Then he cursed and skidded to a stop and ran back.

Nidal was coming awake, moaning as he touched his torn nose with his bloody, trembling fingers. Eckstein straddled him, shoved a glove inside his jacket, yanked out the bank envelope and looked down and hissed, "Fuck you, my good man," and he ran.

He hit the alleyway's intersection at a flat-out sprint just as a dark grey Opel Cadet screeched to a stop in front of him. The rear door flew open, and he saw Baum's face and he jumped inside as the car lurched forward and he slammed back into the seat and the door clanged shut. Yaakov was driving and for a moment they raced parallel to the promenade and then made a hard screaming left. Nava was in front, gripping the dashboard and apparently praying. Eckstein tore off his scarf and collapsed back in the seat as he tried to recall the simple act of breathing.

"Did you get it?" Benni asked. He was speaking English.

"Yes." Eckstein's eyes were closed, and he heard a police siren somewhere, but it wasn't behind them.

"Where's the money?"

"I took it back. And thank you for your concern. I'm fine."

Benni ignored that. "Good boy. Sylvia will be pleased."

Sylvia was the department comptroller and a holy terror when it came to expenses. Behind her back they called her Arafat.

Eckstein heard a window slide down and he smelled blessed rain. He heard the strike of a match, and he opened his eyes and Baum handed him a cigarette. He took a long drag and tried not to think about how close he'd come to never smoking again.

"So, Eytan." Benni turned in his seat and raised his bulbous nose. "How did you fuck this one up?"

"It was a movie ticket." Eckstein rolled his own window down and looked at the buildings flashing by. The rain felt good on his face. "Apparently, the theater is closed."

For a moment Benni said nothing, and then he began to laugh. In a state of repose, he resembled the Italian dictator, Benito Mussolini, but in a state of mirth his face transformed into that of a jolly elf. He couldn't stop himself and his belly jiggled and his face flushed pink.

"Amateur!" he roared, and he slapped Eckstein's knee as they hit the highway ramp, bounced up onto the A4, and kept on going straight for Budapest.

About the Author

STEVEN HARTOV is the coauthor of the *New York Times* bestseller *In the Company of Heroes*, as well as *The Soul of a Thief* and *The Last of the Seven*. For six years he served as editor in chief of Special Operations Report, and has appeared on CNN, MSNBC, Fox, and the History Channel. A former Merchant Marine sailor, Israel Defense Forces paratrooper, and task force commander in the New York Guard, his works are recommended readings by the U.S. Army War College.

Acknowledgements

With gratitude to my faithful, brilliant, and tireless publicist, Lis Malone. And much thanks to 4pm Press for their fine design, as well as enduring an author's capricious state of mind.